W9-BMT-636

THE
SNOOPY
SHOW

A SNOOPY TALE

by Charles M. Schulz
Based on *The Snoopy Show* episode "A Snoopy Tale"
written by Miles Smith
Adapted by Patty Michaels

X Z
I R
M

Ready-to-Read

Simon Spotlight
New York   London   Toronto   Sydney   New Delhi

SIMON SPOTLIGHT

An imprint of Simon & Schuster Children's Publishing Division

1230 Avenue of the Americas, New York, New York 10020

This Simon Spotlight edition August 2021

Peanuts and all related titles, logos, and characters are trademarks of Peanuts Worldwide LLC © 2021 Peanuts Worldwide LLC.

SIMON SPOTLIGHT, READY-TO-READ, and colophon are registered trademarks of Simon & Schuster, Inc. For information about special discounts for bulk purchases, please contact Simon & Schuster Special Sales at 1-866-506-1949 or business@simonandschuster.com.

Manufactured in the United States of America 0721 LAK

10 9 8 7 6 5 4 3 2 1

ISBN 978-1-5344-8554-9 (hc)

ISBN 978-1-5344-8553-2 (pbk)

ISBN 978-1-5344-8555-6 (ebook)

It was a sunny day,
and Snoopy was hard at work
writing a book!

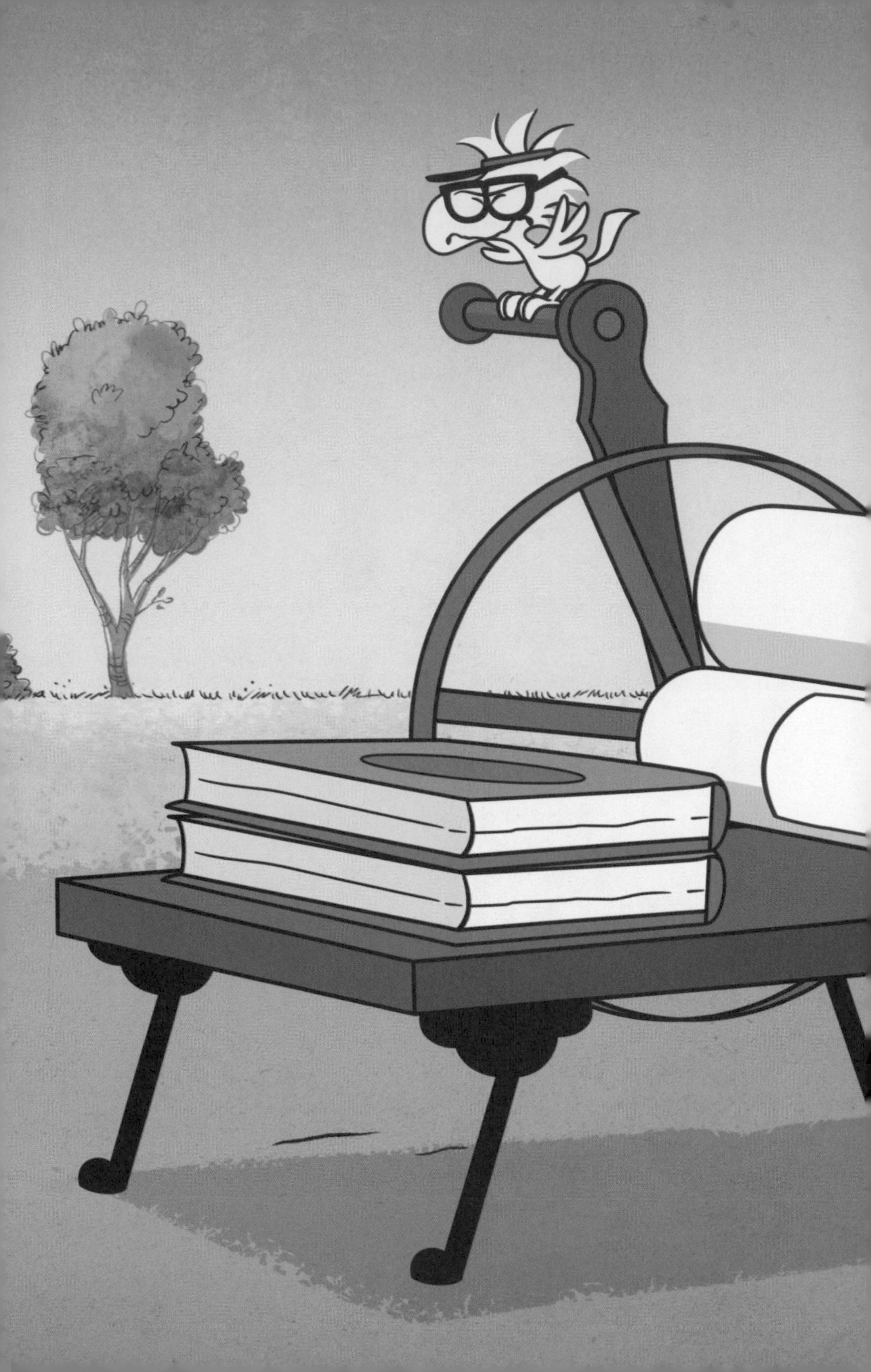

Woodstock and the Beagle
Scouts helped Snoopy put
all the pages together.
Snoopy was so excited
to share his story!

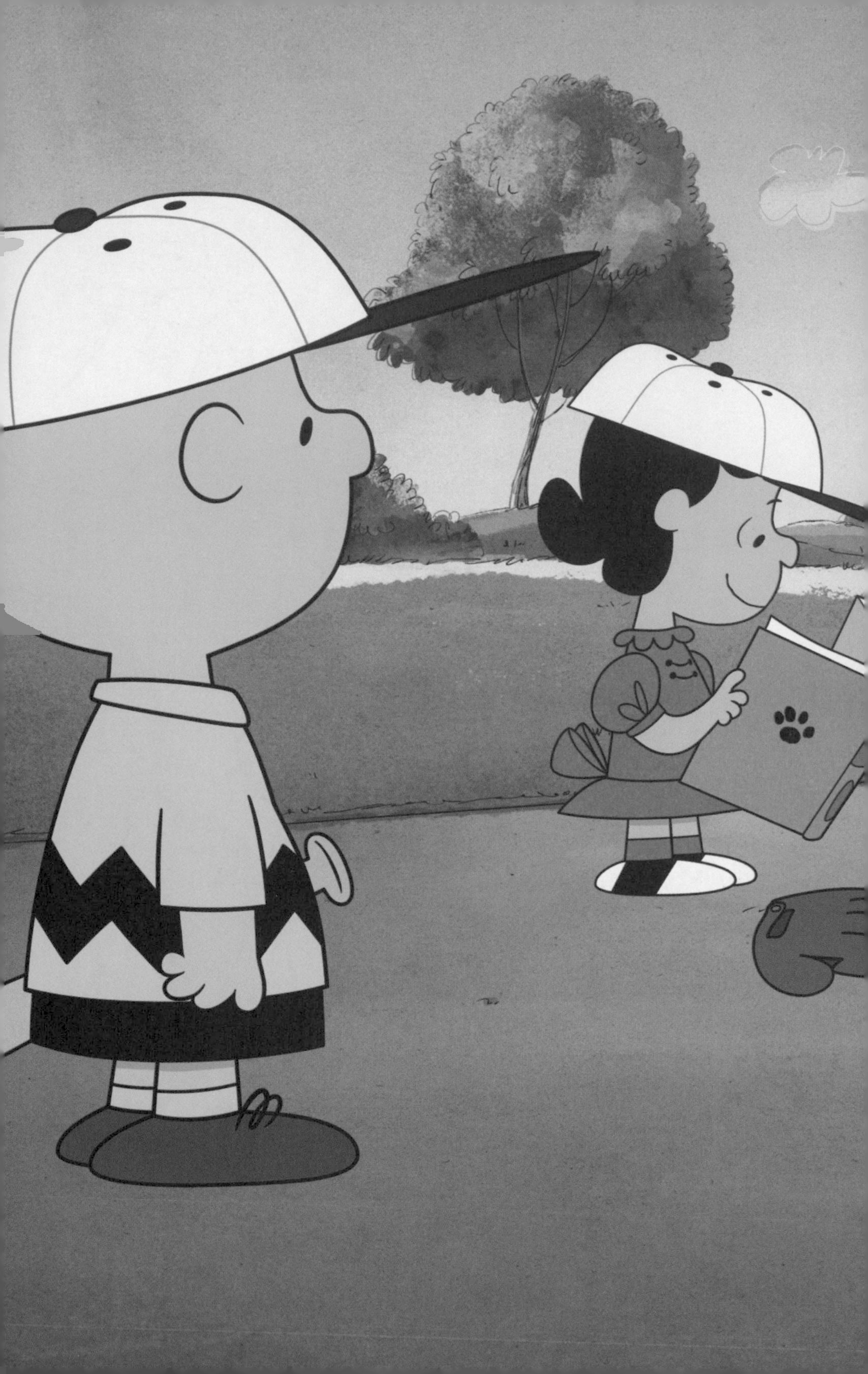

Later, Charlie Brown went to play baseball with his friends.
But no one was paying attention to the game.

"You won't believe it, but that dog of yours has written his autobiography!" Marcie said.

"I never knew Snoopy was born in the Southwest," Franklin said.

"Wait a minute!"
Charlie Brown exclaimed.
"Snoopy wasn't born in the
Southwest. He was born at
the Daisy Hill Puppy Farm!"

Lucy frowned.
"I like the cowboy story better,"
she said.

"What else is in that book?"
Charlie Brown wondered.

"*Chapter Two. Even as a puppy, I had style and knew how to make a big entrance,*" Linus read.

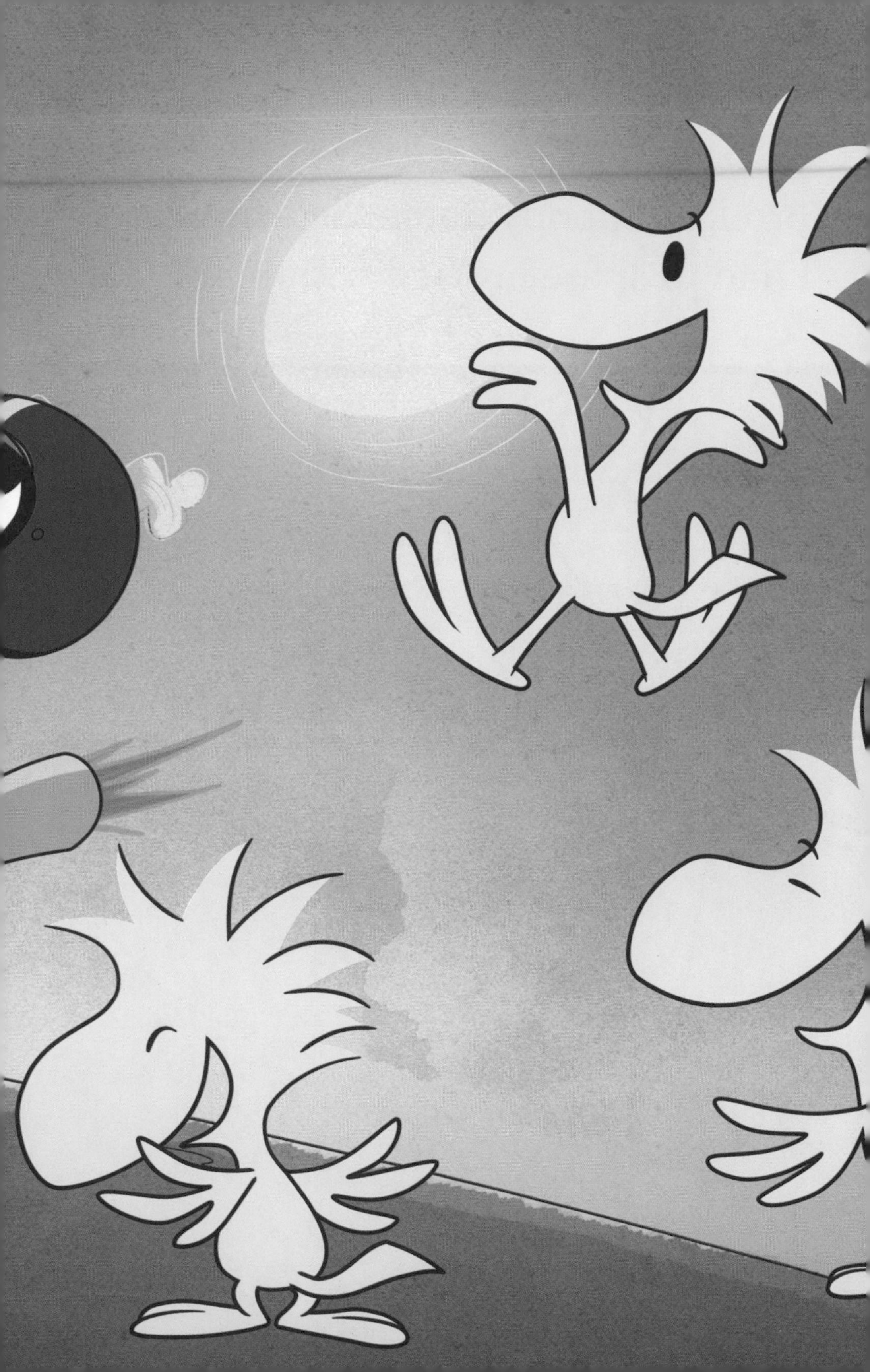

"That's not how it happened at all,"
Charlie Brown said. "When I first
brought Snoopy home, he was scared!
I had to share my bed with him!"

Charlie Brown told his side of the story, exactly as he remembered it.

First, Charlie Brown got Snoopy his own doghouse. Snoopy hopped on top of the roof and smiled.

Then he fell asleep!
"I suppose sleeping on the roof
can be nice too," Charlie Brown said.

Next, Charlie Brown remembered when he tried to teach Snoopy some tricks. "Okay, Snoopy. We'll start with a simple command. Ready? Sit!"

Charlie Brown sighed.
"Let's try another one," he said.
"Shake!"
Snoopy left the room.
A few moments later,
he returned with a milkshake!

"You're supposed to follow my commands like a regular dog, and if you do, I'll give you a doggy treat,"
Charlie Brown told Snoopy.

Snoopy walked over to the kitchen and put a pizza in the oven. When it was ready, he took a big bite and grinned. Clearly, Snoopy knew how to get his own treats!

"The point is, I trained Snoopy,"
Charlie Brown said.

Sally looked through the book. "Well, it's not in the book, big brother. In fact, there's no mention of you at all."

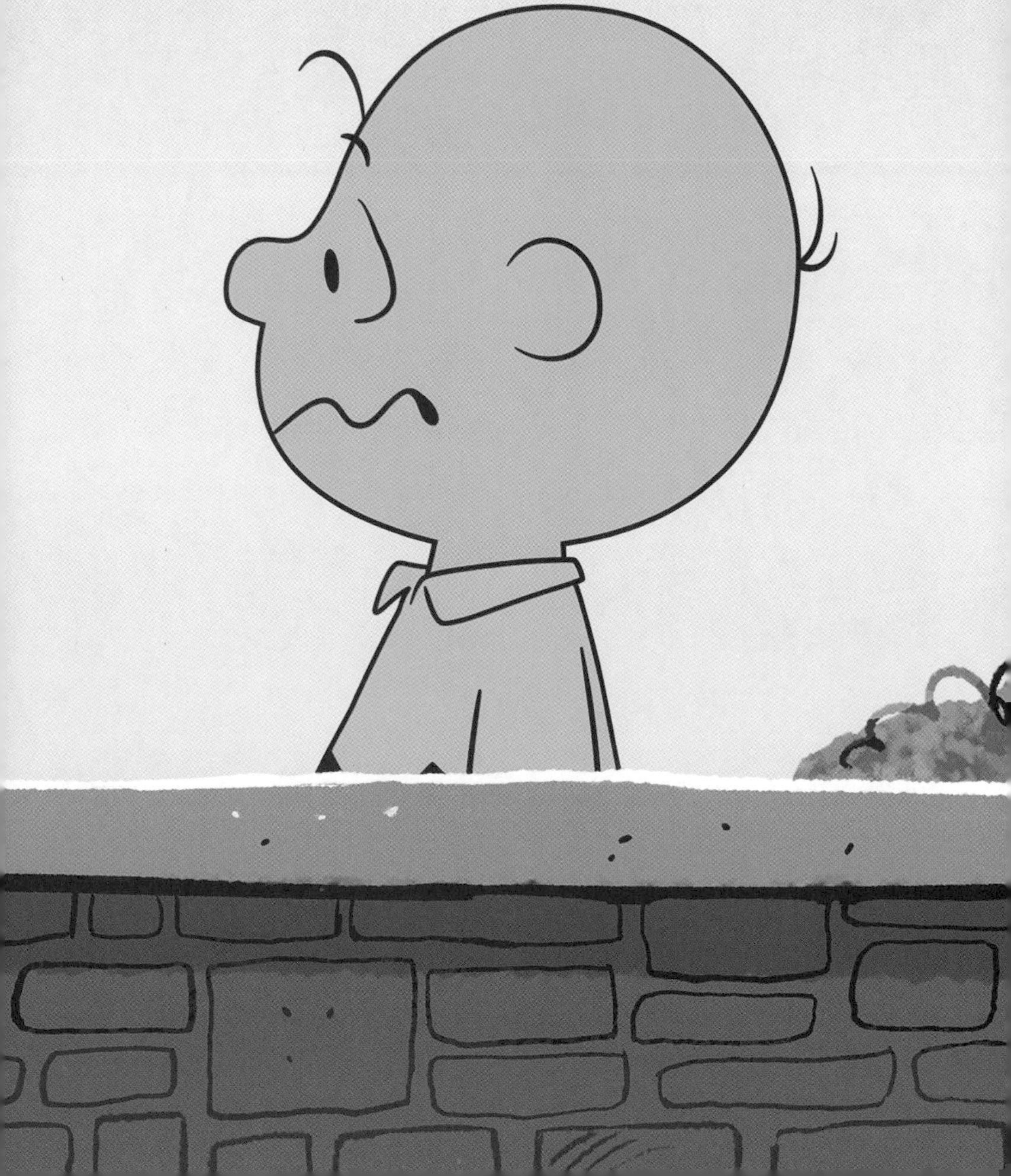

"That's impossible!"
Charlie Brown said.

He marched over to Snoopy,
who was busy signing autographs.

"Snoopy, I'm happy you wrote a book," Charlie Brown said. "But why didn't you even mention me? You're supposed to be my best friend."

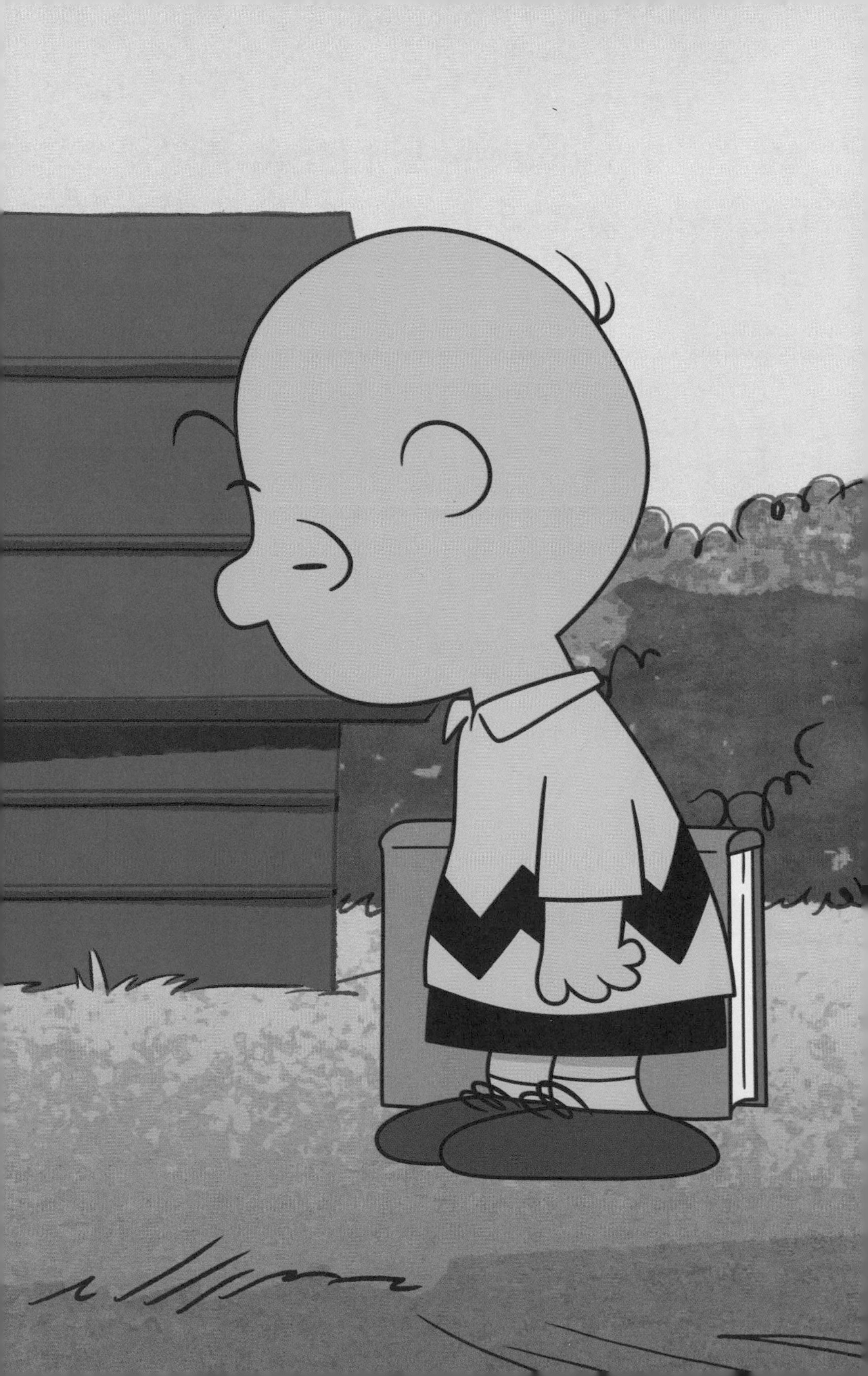

Snoopy opened the book to the
first page and pointed.

"Dedicated to that Round-Headed Kid who brings me dinner," Charlie Brown read aloud.

"That's me!" Charlie Brown exclaimed.
"You dedicated it to *me*!
Thanks, Snoopy!"

Charlie Brown hugged his
best friend, Snoopy.

Charlie Brown smiled. He was happy to know that Snoopy's story had started with him!

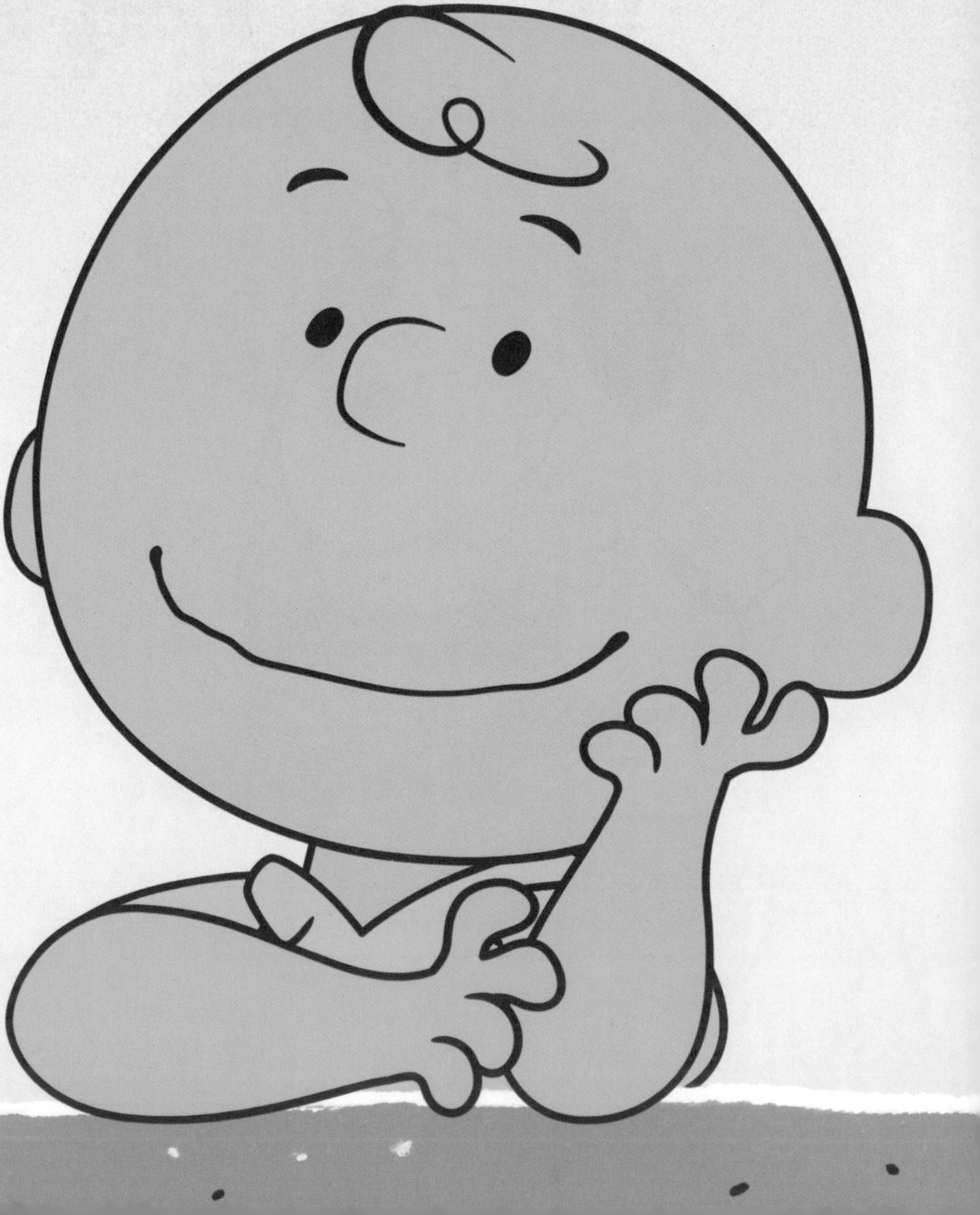